Text copyright © 1998 by Eleanor Walsh Meyer
Illustrations copyright © 1998 by Vlad Guzner

Library of Congress catalog card number: 97-62299
Printed in Hong Kong
Designed by Bretton Clark
First edition, 1998

The Keeper
of Ugly
Sounds

To Wyatt—
Enjoy—
Eleana Walsh Meyer

To my parents, Gabrielle and Tom Walsh,
in whose home ugly sounds were seldom heard

⁓E.W.M.

To Catherine

⁓V.G.

The Keeper of Ugly Sounds

Eleanor Walsh Meyer ~ Illustrated by Vlad Guzner

WINSLOW PRESS

nce upon a time, a little boy was born in a house only two inches shorter than a castle. The house perched straight on top of a just-right hill.~twenty runs, six skips, and a hop from the Sleepy Village. Tall pines hummed their tree songs all about the place, and a crystal blue river, full of fat and friendly fish, ran busily below.

The boy's parents were terribly excited when he arrived, for he was their first child. Every spare minute, they ran into the nursery, tickling him under the chin as they made happy mother and father noises over him in his crib. But it was strange, for instead of gurgling~or at least trying to smile a little~the boy would just glurp back at them in a very crabby fashion.

At first his parents thought he was sick, or perhaps in need of a bit more food. So they sent for doctors, who came from Closeby and Faraway.

"No, no! There's not a single thing wrong with his insides," the doctors all said. "He just wants what he wants when he wants it!"

As he grew older, the boy got worse. If he couldn't have his way, he shrieked. He shouted when other people were talking. He howled and howled when he had to go to bed. And no matter what they were having for meals, he fussed about it.

Jars of cotton were placed in every room of the house, for whenever he'd start up, everyone rushed to stuff their ears. Even in the summertime, the windows were fastened tight because the Sleepy Villagers complained about the noise.

The boy's parents tried scoldings and punishments of all sorts. Still, the commotion he made was so dreadful that the cook, the maid, the nurse, and the gardener all dashed out of the house, arms over their heads, promising never to come back again. No matter what!

Villagers couldn't Sleep!

INTERVIEW WITH BABYSITTER

One fine morning, the boy was out on the lawn, muttering a complainy grumble for no reason at all, when a strange sprout of a man appeared. He wore wood-colored britches topped by a bright checkered vest, a white shirt, and a neat bow tie at his neck. From the side of his peaked green hat an orange feather—the length of a tree branch—blew jauntily in the breeze.

The little man said not a word. Instead, he grabbed the boy by the arm and pulled him off. The boy's yowls and howls were piercing, but the wee man didn't seem to hear. He just kept tugging the boy down the just-right hill, past the busy river, through the Sleepy Village, and into the midst of a twisty, snarly forest.

When they arrived in front of a squatty brown hut, the little man let go of the boy's arm.

"Now, my little fellow," he said in a voice that sounded like the drone of a hummingbird. "You are going to be the Keeper of Ugly Sounds. The bad-tempered noises people make all over the world end up here. They must be put in bags and tied up tight so they never get loose again. As you make so many of the sounds yourself, I'm certain you'll be an excellent Keeper."

Then, faster than the wind blows across a stormy sky, the little man was gone.

The tangled forest was a terrible place.
Ugly sounds were lying all about〜the grunts
grunting, the moans moaning, and the
shrieks shrieking.

The boy tried to get out of the forest
to the north, toward the south, that way and
this way. But whichever path he took led him
swiftly back〜smack in front of the
squatty brown hut.

Finally, because the sounds were so bothersome that he couldn't stand the racket any longer, he had to do what the small man had said.

What a job it was! Every single second, the boy was busy. He had to be sure that the cries went into the Cry Bag, the sighs into the Sigh Bag, and all the other ugly sounds into the right ugly-sound bag. Sometimes, but not often (because he learned to be extremely careful), the boy got mixed up and put a scream into a Groan Bag, and then the uproar was horrible.

Day after day, the boy was up ever so late, sorting the sounds, tying the bags up tight, and storing them in the cellar of the squatty brown hut. And when the last star was still blinking good-night to day, he had to jump out of bed, for a whole new pile of sounds had arrived and needed to be sorted out.

Once a week, when the bags were full (for ugly sounds weigh hardly a thing), the boy loaded them on to a creaky cart and hauled them to the Lake With No Bottom. Once there, he dumped the bags into the water with a huge stone tied to each one so they couldn't possibly float back to the top. When he was finished, the boy would rush back to the hut and start filling new bags with sounds.

Smudgy circles soon appeared under the boy's eyes. His ears became swollen and red because he could never remove the large rubber plugs he now wore. He almost never had time to eat enough, and soon his pants got so big for him that he was obliged to use safety pins and a piece of rope to hold them up.

It seemed to the boy that he'd been in the snarly, twisty forest forever when one day, while he was rushing back from the Lake With No Bottom, he suddenly sobbed aloud.

"Oh dear! How could I have ever made those ugly noises? If only I had known how truly terrible they sounded, I never would have made even the littlest one."

He stopped a minute to brush away his tears and to scratch a tickle under his nose. The tickle, the boy discovered, was caused by the large orange feather belonging to the peaked green hat that rested on the head of the whimsy man.

"It's too bad," the man sighed, his hummingbird drone sounding very sad. "After what you just said, I can't let you stay here. And you've been doing such a fine job. Remarkably fine. But to be the Keeper of Ugly Sounds, you have to *like* bad noises. Now you've gone and changed your mind! Someone else will have to take your place."

And in a wink they were out of the forest, through the Sleepy Village, past the busy river, and back on top of the just-right hill. The little boy was home! He turned to his companion, but not the faintest trace of an orange feather was in sight, so the boy raced into the house.

His mother and father were thrilled to see him, for they had worried and worried. And when they found how he had changed, they hugged him, hugged each other, and made happy mother and father noises for the first time since he was a baby.

Up went the windows! Out went
the jars of cotton! Back came the
cook, the maid, the nurse, and the
gardener. Every nook and cranny of
the house was filled with chuckles and
laughs and giggles and purrs. In fact,
people came from all over to visit, because
it was such a happy place to stay.

And from that time on, not even the slightest ugly sound was ever heard in the house only two inches shorter than a castle.

 The End